TO FIND
TREASURE
IN THE MOUNTAINS

Francine Rockey

ILLUSTRATED BY Kendra Binney

YOSEMITE CONSERVANCY
Yosemite National Park

YOSEMITE
CONSERVANCY.
yosemite.org

Yosemite Conservancy inspires people to support projects and
programs that preserve Yosemite and enrich the visitor experience.

Library of Congress Cataloging-in-Publication Data

Names: Rockey, Francine, author. | Binney. Kendra. illustrator.
Title: To find treasure in the mountains / Francine Rockey ; illustrated by Kendra Binney.
Description: Yosemite National Park : Yosemite Conservancy. [2022] |
     Audience: Ages 4-6. | Audience: Grades K-1. | Summary: Three children
     find different treasures in nature as they spend a day following a trail
     in the woods.
Identifiers: LCCN 2021050514 (print) | LCCN 2021050515 (ebook) | ISBN
     9781951179168 (hardcover) | ISBN 9781951179229 (epub)
Subjects: CYAC: Hiking--Fiction. | Nature--Fiction.
Classification: LCC PZ7.1.R639525 To 2022 (print) | LCC PZ7.1.R639525
     (ebook) | DDC [E]--dc23
LC record available at https://lccn.loc.gov/2021050514

LC ebook record available at https://lccn.loc.gov/2021050515

Design by Katie Jennings Campbell

Printed in China by Toppan Leefung

1 2 3 4 5 6 — 26 25 24 23 22

MIX
Paper from
responsible sources
FSC® C104723
www.fsc.org

For Ken, Beau, and Levi,
who treasure the trail with me
— F. R.

For Maddie, Isaac, and Jacob
— K. B.

If you want to find treasure

in the mountains, you don't need a
magical fairy or a wise, wand-waving wizard.
You don't even need a pan to sift for gold
or a pirate map with X marking the spot.

All you need to find treasure here
is a sturdy pair of shoes.
And to remember which way is away
and which way is home.
Once your sturdy shoes are on tight
and your which-ways are set right,
start stepping toward away.

Down that trail
you'll find...

treasure!

This trail leads there too.
All steps into the wild
lead to treasure.

Listen to the Steller's jay screech.
Place your hand on the rough red bark of the
great evergreen and hear the wind whisper...

treasure.

The path can twist and dip and—whoa!
It's okay.
Even seasoned treasure seekers
sometimes stumble.

Plus, when you're down with the wildflowers and pine needles,
you can go eye to eye with grasshoppers.

Eye to eye with a grasshopper,
you'll be very close to treasure!

Watch the tiny ant carry a tremendous twig on its back.
You, too, are stronger than you appear.

The doe leaps over the creek.
The creek trickling beneath burbles,

treasure!

Sit so still the painted lady butterfly
believes your ear is a flower petal.

The lizard's blue belly soaks
up sunlight like sapphires.
Soak up sunshine with the lizard.

Trace the glitter lines up and up along the granite.
You see, this treasure is bigger than boulders.

There are slick spots and steep steps
and hard-to-reach places,
but you can be as brave as a black bear
and as steady as a mountain lion.

Test your footing,
trust your strength,
and try, and try,
and
yes!

Now open your eyes even wider,
like the great gray owl,
and turn your head to look up
and down and all around.

You've found **treasure!**

It is
all treasure.

Treasure it.

Now, remember which
way is home?
Step toward home.

You say you want to
keep the treasure?

You will!

INSPIRATION

I was six years old, visiting my aunt's cabin, when I first stepped on a winding trail through the woods. It was a long time ago, yet I remember it with perfect precision. I felt like Alice in Wonderland and Dorothy in Oz, but I didn't need a rabbit hole or a tornado. The trail was a real-world portal to enchantment. It still is!

I carry folded between the pages of my notebook a beloved Mary Oliver quote: "Inside the river there is an unfinishable story / and you are somewhere in it." I've felt this connection since that first twisting trail. Nature jolts us into the joy of the moment. We're revived by the soapy scent of a freesia bloom, refreshed by a mountain's face changing with the sunset, dazzled by dewdrops like diamonds on spiderwebs. Each marvel feels like finding a gold coin on the ground—but better.

And it's not just the poets who know. Doctors and other scientists study and share the benefits of time outdoors. Architects use the power of biophilia (the comfort we feel in nature) when they place plant life in their plans for schools and other buildings. Being in the open air makes us happier, healthier, and kinder. So, let's get outside and find a moment to treasure!

—F. R.